TERRY DEARY'S TALES

PIRATES AND PERIL

Illustrated by Helen Flook

A & C BLACK
AN IMPRINT OF BLOOMSBURY
LONDON NEW DELHI NEW YORK SYDNEY

First published by
A & C Black, an imprint of Bloomsbury Publishing plc
50 Bedford Square
London WC1B 3DP

www.bloomsbury.com

ISBN 978-1-4729-0671-7

Printed and Bound by CPI Group (UK) Ltd, Croydon CR0 4YY

1 3 5 7 9 10 8 6 4 2

TERRY DEARY'S
PIRATE TALES

The Pirate Captain

Illustrated by Helen Flook

A & C BLACK
AN IMPRINT OF BLOOMSBURY
LONDON NEW DELHI NEW YORK SYDNEY

Chapter One
Seas and Slaughter

The North Atlantic, 1726

Captain Fly was a small man. Not as small as a fly, of course, but not much larger than a boy.

"I am the terror of the Atlantic Ocean!" he boasted. "In fact, I may be the greatest terror of the seven seas!"

"What seas are those, then, Captain?" his greasy-haired, bare-footed, bear-brained, bullying mate Mr Blood wanted to know.

"Seas?"

"Yes, Captain Fly. What are the *seven* seas?" Blood asked.

"Well, there's the North Atlantic... and the *South* Atlantic, of course."

"Of course," his ugly friend Mr Slaughter nodded. "But what about the other five?"

"The Pacific Ocean... and that makes *seven*."

"Three," Mr Blood corrected.

Fly turned as red as a cockerel's comb. He waved his short, dirty fingers under Blood's nose and counted. "North... one... Atlantic... two... South... three... Atlantic... four... The... five... Pacific... six... Ocean... seven. Seven seas, *see*?"

"Suppose," Mr Blood grumbled.

"Suppose?" Captain Fly sneered. "Nobody argues with William Fly. I was a boxing champion, you know."

"I know."

"And I'll batter anybody that argues with me." The captain turned suddenly towards Slaughter. "You're bigger than me, Slaughter, but I could batter you."

He waved a fist under the sailor's broken nose. "I'm fast. Fast Fly they used to call me in the boxing ring. Champion of America, I was. Fast Fly."

"Too fast for me, Captain," Slaughter chuckled. "Too fast for any man on the three seas."

"Seven seas," Fly said.

"Yes, them as well."

Captain Fly turned back to Blood. "Now fetch the prisoners on deck. It's time I gave them their orders."

Chapter Two
Blood and Batter

Mr Blood opened a hatch in the deck of the rolling ship. Five men and a boy blinked in the sunlight.

"Up on deck, you scurvy lot. Captain Fly wants to give you your orders."

The men had been crowded into a small space for over an hour and they were stiff.

"Hurry it up," Seaman Slaughter shouted. "Nobody keeps Captain Fly waiting... or, if they do, he batters them. Batter, batter, batter," Slaughter said, and made punching movements with his fat fists.

Most of the prisoners looked afraid. But one man stood taller than the rest and he just looked amused. He held a trembling skinny boy by the hand and muttered,

"It'll be all right, young Arthur. I'll not let them hurt you."

Slaughter pushed them into a line. "Right, prisoners. Silence while Captain Fly speaks."

Fly climbed up onto the aft deck so he could look down his twisted nose at the miserable men. He gave a black-toothed grin. "You're a lucky bunch, you are. When we captured your ship this morning, we took your tobacco load and then we sank the old tub. Any other pirate would have sunk you with it. But not me. Not Captain Fly. I'm too kind for that."

The tall prisoner stepped forward. "A kind man wouldn't have robbed us in the first place," he said.

Fly turned purple with anger. "Nobody argues with William Fly. I was a boxing champion, you know, and I'll batter anyone that argues with me. What's your name?"

"Captain Jed Atkinson," the tall man said. "I'm captain of the ship your villains just sank."

Fly threw back his head and laughed a mad laugh. "Ha! Ha! Hahhhhh! You are not *captain* any longer. There's room for only *one* captain on a ship, and the captain of *Fame's Revenge* is me. And if anyone ever calls *you* captain on board *my* ship, I'll feed him to the sharks. Understand?"

"There are not many sharks on the east coast of America," Jed Atkinson said quietly.

Captain Fly pretended he hadn't heard. "As I was saying, I am the kindest pirate you'll ever have the good luck to meet. My ship is short of crew, and you are sailors, so I kept you alive to help me."

"What happened to the rest of your crew?" the boy said in a trembling voice. "Did you feed them to the sharks?"

Fly glared at him. "No. No... they got so rich with their share of the treasure, they retired. And that's what *you* will do, too. Serve me for a year, and I'll make you as rich as a king. But try to escape, and I'll batter you."

"He'll batter you. Batter, batter, batter," Seaman Slaughter said, and laughed. "Hur, hur, hur!"

Chapter Three
Slaves and Sharks

"We're slaves," young Arthur groaned. His red-brown hair had been cut with a blunt knife and it was as shaggy as a bear.

"Slaves?" Jed smiled. "For a while..."

"For ever," the boy said.

Jed hauled on the ropes to raise the sail and head north. The coast of North Carolina was a grey-green smudge on the horizon. "We have a lot going for us, Arthur."

"What? He's a champion boxer... we can't fight him. Even if we did, he has Blood and Slaughter to help him. And they have pistols."

The tall man tied the rope and turned to the boy. "No sailor can stay at sea for ever. He has to go into port at least once a month. There'll be lots of chances to escape."

"But Blood and Slaughter..."

"...are as stupid as William Fly. We'll have lots of chances to trick them."

Arthur's face brightened and he wiped away the tears. "When, Captain Atkinson?"

"Don't call me captain, remember? Call me Jed."

"Yes, Captain," the boy promised. "What's your plan?"

"The first part of the plan is to work hard. Get Fly to trust us. Do exactly what he says. Look as if we're happy," Jed said.

"And rob other ships? But the navy might catch us and hang us along with the real pirates," Arthur sighed.

"We don't have a lot of choice. If we refuse to help, he'll throw us overboard... to feed the sharks that aren't there."

"And the second part of your plan?"

"Wait and see. I'll tell you when the time comes."

"What are you two muttering about?" Seaman Slaughter asked as he marched down the deck.

Arthur stepped forward to meet him. "We were just saying how lucky we are to have been captured by you and Captain Fly. We can't wait to start boarding ships and getting rich."

"Can't you?" the ugly sailor grunted.

"Captain Fly is the greatest pirate to sail the Atlantic," Jed Atkinson put in.

"The greatest to sail the seven seas," Slaughter told him.

"What seas are those?" Arthur asked.

"Erm... North Atlantic, South Atlantic and the Pacific Ocean," Slaughter told him.

"That's only three," Arthur said.

Slaughter shook his head. "Captain Fly says it's seven, so it must be seven," he said, and walked away.

Arthur looked at Jed Atkinson. "You're right, Captain – about as stupid as they come."

Chapter Four
Sails and Sandbanks

The first ship that young Arthur robbed was a cutter not much larger than the rowing boat of *Fame's Revenge*. It was sailing close to the shore with sacks of grain and packets of food on deck.

The skipper saw *Fame's Revenge* heading towards him and tried to raise more sail. "Blow him out of the water!" Captain Fly screeched.

His crew ran towards the three cannon he had on the deck and pulled them to the side of the schooner.

Jed Atkinson spoke quietly. "If you sink him, you won't get his cargo, Captain Fly."

"I know that," the pirate replied. He turned to the men hauling the cannon.

"Don't be so stupid – if we sink him, we won't get his cargo – put on more sail. Raise the main gaff topsail," he ordered.

The men let go of the cannon, which started to roll across the slippery deck and crunch into the side. The sailors scrambled over an untidy tangle of ropes and sails and got in one another's way.

Arthur looked at Jed. "He's not a very good sailor, is he?"

"Hopeless," the tall man agreed.

The cutter was starting to sail away. Captain Fly was jumping up and down on the spot. "Get that mainsail up. He's escaping."

"I thought you said the main gaff topsail," Slaughter reminded him.

"Never mind what I said... just do it."

"Urrrr?" Blood grunted.

Suddenly, Jed Atkinson stepped towards the main mast and picked up a rope. He turned to the men that had sailed with him on his own ship. "Muller and Finch, Adams and Bishop... get these ropes sorted. Untie the sails in the right order."

"Yes, Captain Atkinson," Jan Muller said with a grin and the sailors worked quickly like the team they used to be.

"Take this rope, Slaughter," Jed said calmly. "You, Blood, haul this mainsail first... that's right... now, Slaughter, the main gaff topsail's free... it'll go up next."

Slaughter smiled a green-toothed smile. "So it does, Captain."

"He's not a captain!" Fly raged. "I told you not to call him captain or you'll be thrown over the side."

"I'll throw myself over the side when we're on the beach," Slaughter promised. "Look, Captain Fly, we're getting closer to the cutter now."

"And we're getting closer to the sandbanks," Jed said. "Take the rudder, Arthur," he ordered the red-haired boy. "Steer to starboard... that's the way. I know these waters, and we'll run aground in a ship this big. The captain of the cutter knows that. He's trying to lead us into a trap."

"A trap, a trap!" Fly shrieked. "I knew it. Just as well you have me to save your scurvy lives!" he cried.

"We're in a deep channel now," Jed Atkinson said a few minutes later. "Hard to port, Arthur, and we'll cut him off. He'll have to stop."

"Cut off the cutter... cutter him off," Fly screamed, and ran to the bow of his schooner to watch as they neared the trading ship. The victim began to run down his sails and slow down, defeated.

"Now lower the sails," Jed shouted to his crew. "That's the way... gaff topsail first... mainsail next. Gently to starboard, Arthur."

Fame's Revenge drifted alongside the cutter and the glum trader threw a line to Slaughter, who hauled the two ships side by side.

"I did it," Fly crowed. "I did it!"

Chapter Five
Pancakes and Poverty

"What do you have on board?" Captain Fly called to the skipper of the cutter.

The miserable man and his three gloomy crew looked up. "Supplies for my shop in Wilmington... not much. I can't afford much. Just a couple of sacks of cornflour, salt, butter, a barrel of wine and one of molasses."

"What's molasses?" Captain Fly asked.

"It's what you call treacle back in England," Slaughter explained.

"Not much of a treasure," Arthur muttered, a little too loudly.

"We'll eat well for a week," Fly said angrily.

Blood scratched his head through greasy hair and pulled out a louse. "Cornflour and treacle? We can't eat cornflour and treacle."

"No… no…" Captain Fly huffed. "We bake the cornflour into bread."

"There isn't an oven on this schooner, Captain Fly," Slaughter reminded him.

Just as Fly was about to explode, Jed stepped forward. "Young Arthur was the galley boy on our ship. He can turn cornflour into wonderful pancakes over the hotplate."

31

"Ha! See?" Fly smirked. "We can have pancakes... lovely with treacle, they are. My mum used to fry them back in Bristol. Lovely. Now, load them onto *Fame's Revenge*," he ordered.

That evening, the schooner sat at anchor and the crew ate a mountain of pancakes that Arthur made. They sat around the main mast and washed the meal down with wine.

Jed turned to Captain Fly. "So how did you get into pirating, Captain?" he asked.

Fly breathed in deeply so his skinny chest blew out like a bullfrog's. "I gave up boxing in Bristol to join a slave-trader, Captain Green. We bought slaves in Africa and sold them in Jamaica for ten times the price."

"A good deal," Jed said and gave a glance of disgust towards Arthur.

"It would have been better if so many slaves hadn't died on the trip," Fly spat.

"But Captain Green was a cruel man. He had his crew flogged at the drop of a hat."

"Is that where you learned to be cruel?" Arthur asked.

Fly's eyes glowed as he remembered. "One night, my friends, Blood and Slaughter, dropped old Green on an island in the Atlantic and I took over *Fame's Revenge*. I gave up the slaving – all those Atlantic storms were ruining my ship. I decided to pirate off the coast of Carolina – there are so many little ships that run up and down from Dismal Swamp down to Cape Fear. It's an easy life."

"Bullying little ships and driving them into poverty," Jed said quietly.

"That was two weeks ago, Atkinson, and you were my first prize. Easy," Fly crowed.

"Easy when you have a couple of cannon," Jed agreed.

"Easy," Fly nodded and his head fell forward onto his chest. He snored.

When the wine sent Blood and Slaughter to sleep, too, Jed Atkinson wandered to check the anchor chain at the front. When he was sure Fly's crew were not going to wake up, he gave a small signal for his own men to join him. Muller and Finch, Adams and Bishop crept forward with young Arthur.

"Yes?" Dick Adams asked quietly. "Do you have a plan to get us off this Hell-ship?"

"I have a plan," their true captain replied.

Arthur felt a glow of happiness warm him deep inside.

Chapter Six
Flag and Flight

Next morning was cool and windy. *Fame's Revenge* rocked and creaked as it wallowed in the water, waiting. Captain Fly was too lazy to sail out to seek his victims.

"We sit here and let them come to us," he told his crew. "That's what a great pirate would do. Pass me a pancake, young Arthur."

He was eating his third pancake of the morning and grease was dribbling into his scrawny beard when Muller called down from the top of the mast, "Brig trading ship to the east, Captain Fly."

Fly looked around at the crew. "Well? What are you waiting for?"

"For orders, Captain Fly," Dick Adams told him.

Fly shook his ugly head. "Run a flag to the top of the mast. A flag of distress to show we're in trouble," he said slowly, as if he were talking to a child.

"But we aren't in trouble, Captain," Slaughter said.

Fly rolled his eyes. "No, but the brig will come to our rescue. As soon as she comes alongside, we'll capture her, understand?"

"No," Slaughter said.

"It's... a... *trick*, Slaughter. Saves us the trouble of chasing the brig."

"Oh, I see," Blood grinned. "Clever Captain Fly. A trick!"

"Oh, I get it," Slaughter said with a gap-toothed smile. "Hur! Hur! Hur!"

Seaman Bishop found a white flag with a red cross. He tied it to a rope and pulled till the flag slid up the mast.

The crew watched as the brig drew closer. As soon as it was half a mile away, it raised its sails and turned away.

"What's happening?" Fly cried.

"He's running away from us, Captain," Blood replied.

"But we need help!" Fly wailed.

"No, we don't," Slaughter argued.

"He *thinks* we do," the captain raged.

Jed Atkinson sighed. "That's Martin Paris's ship – he's not a fool. He knows it's a trick."

Fly jumped to his feet. "After him, Atkinson. After him. Catch him. Blow him out of the water. Hurry!"

Jed Atkinson took command. He gave the orders and turned *Fame's Revenge* to race after the brig.

"I'll kill them," Fly shouted. "I'll batter them all when I catch them."

Fame's Revenge reared up like a wild horse and set off on the chase.

Chapter Seven
Fame and Fortune

Jed Atkinson made sure *Fame's Revenge* soon caught Martin Paris's brig.

Captain Fly ran across the deck and stood behind a loaded cannon. "Surrender... surrender or die!" he called and waved a lighted fuse over the cannon.

Captain Martin Paris spread his hands. "What do you want?" he asked.

"All your gold and all your silver. Your pistols... and your pancakes," the little Englishman cried.

Paris shook his head sadly. "If you bring your ship too close, we'll break up... the sea's too rough today. You'll have to send over a rowing boat to pick up our money," he called back. The captain wore his grey hair pulled back into a pigtail that was made stiff with tar.

"Lower the boat, Adams and Bishop," Fly ordered. "Row across and rob their riches."

Adams and Bishop moved slowly towards the rowing boat that was stowed on the deck. They fastened a rope on each end and, with the help of Muller and Finch, they lowered it into the frothing water.

Young Arthur stepped forward quickly. He was trembling. He had to get his part in the plot right. "No, Captain Fly... you can't let Adams and Bishop go. They'll jump onto Captain Paris's ship and escape. You can't trust them."

"Oh, no," Adams groaned, very loud. *Too* loud, Arthur thought. He was acting his part a bit too hard. "Oh, no... that cursed boy has ruined our plan. Our plan to escape."

"Oh, no," Seaman Bishop sighed, even louder.

"Aha!" Captain Fly laughed. "You can't trick a cunning pirate like William Fly, my lads. I saw through your plan. I'm not going to let you row off to freedom."

Adams and Bishop hung their heads and tried to look sad.

"What do we do then?" Slaughter asked.

"Well, it's as clear as the nose on your face, Slaughter," Fly laughed.

There was silence for a moment. Just the slapping of waves against the side of *Fame's Revenge*.

"Well?" Blood asked. "What *do* we do?"

"Ha! Ha! Hahhhhh!" Fly laughed. "What do we do? You're an idiot, Blood." He looked over his shoulder. "Tell him what we do, Jed Atkinson."

Jed gave a soft smile. "Even young Arthur knows what we do. Tell Seaman Blood, lad."

Arthur nodded. "We send Captain Fly's most trusted men across to the brig. Give Slaughter and Blood all the pistols we have and let them row across," the boy told Fly.

"See? Idiot. You and Slaughter row across... here, take my pistol. Don't come back without my fortune."

"*Your* fortune, Captain Fly?" Slaughter said with a frown.

"*Our* fortune, I meant to say. Now hurry. I can't wait to run my fingers through a chest full of gold."

Chapter Eight
Rope and Revenge

Slaughter and Blood climbed down the rope at the side of *Fame's Revenge* and fell into the rowing boat with a clunk. They were clumsy sailors and it took them a while to untangle themselves from the oars and set off towards Martin Paris's ship.

Jed Atkinson walked over to the side of *Fame's Revenge* and waved at Captain Paris. "Hello there, Martin, are you well?"

Paris scowled. "Jed Atkinson turned pirate? I can't believe it!"

"No, Martin, I was a prisoner of Captain Fly. Now I want you to do a small favour, old friend."

"What's that?"

"Sail in to the harbour at Wilmington and tell them we're bringing in the pirate Captain Fly – they can arrest him as soon as we land. We don't want them firing at *Fame's Revenge* when we enter the harbour."

Martin Paris saluted and gave orders for his crew to set sail for Wilmington.

William Fly listened with his mouth open. "Arrest? Arrest me? You can't do that – I'll batter you." He raised his fists and jumped forward. He stepped into a loop of rope that Arthur had laid on the deck.

As Fly's foot went into the noose, Arthur pulled it tight. Fly tripped and fell on his face, roaring with anger. Muller and Finch, Adams and Bishop grabbed an end of the rope, threw it over a spar and hauled on it so Captain Fly was hanging by his foot.

"Blood and Slaughter..." he choked. "Where are Blood and Slaughter, my trusty friends?"

Arthur looked at the upside-down captain who thrashed like a cod on a fishing line. "They're in the Atlantic Ocean in a rowing boat. Captain Paris sailed off before they reached him, and we're sailing off before they can get back here."

"You killed my pirates... they can't row all the way back to Carolina... we're ten miles off the coast!" Fly cried.

"It's all right," Jed Atkinson said with a smile. "We'll hand you over and then we'll send the navy out in a frigate to pick them up. You can all share a cosy jail cell until your trial."

"Ooooh! I don't want to share a cell with those two, they smell like rotting fish. Ooooh! What have I done to deserve this?" the little man wailed.

"Been a pirate," Arthur said. "And that's what happens to all pirates in the end."

Chapter Nine
Cutter and Butter

Jed Atkinson called to Muller and Finch, Adams and Bishop, "Raise the mainsail. Arthur... steady north-west. We'll catch that cutter in half an hour."

Atkinson walked across the deck of *Fame's Revenge* proudly. Captain Fly had sunk his old ship. But the judge had given Jed *Fame's Revenge* as a reward for capturing William Fly.

The little cutter battled through the waves, but it was no match for the big pirate ship and its expert crew. At last the small boat lowered its mast and the captain turned to face his enemy.

"You robbed us last month, William Fly," the man sighed. "We've nothing left worth stealing. Just a few sacks of corn. My family will starve if you rob us again."

Arthur lashed the steering oar tight and joined his captain at the starboard side of the ship. "I'm Captain Jed Atkinson. William Fly's in prison," he shouted across the lapping water.

The captain of the cutter shrugged. "You're still a pirate, whatever you call yourself. And I'm just a shopkeeper that you've ruined. My wife says we'll be eating the leather from our boots if I don't bring these sacks of corn back home safe."

Jed Atkinson grinned. "Fly took two sacks of cornflour from you, salt, butter, a barrel of wine and one of molasses. We're here to give them back." He turned to his crew and ordered them to start unloading supplies from *Fame's Revenge* onto the little cutter.

The shopkeeper watched and his mouth fell open. "My wife will be... she'll be – " he began. But tears choked his throat and he just sniffled as he watched the hold of his ship fill up. Arthur helped load the last of the barrels and sacks before climbing back into *Fame's Revenge*.

Jed waved goodbye, ran back to the steering oar and finally the shopkeeper found his voice. He called across, "A pirate captain that *gives* to his victims? You're like King Arthur and... and his knights of the Round Table. Knights of the sea. What's your name, young sir?"

Arthur threw back his head and laughed the way William Fly had once laughed. "Ha! Ha! Hahhhhh! King Arthur, of course."

And the *Fame's Revenge* headed west into the setting sun to find more good deeds to do.

Epilogue

William Fly was a cruel captain who robbed traders off the American coast in his ship *Fame's Revenge*. The men who sailed his ships were mostly victims he had captured. In the end he was tricked by those prisoners who wanted their own revenge.

Fly was born in England. His life as a pirate started when he led a rebellion on the slave ship *Elizabeth*. The ship had been sailing to West Africa. Fly and his friends threw the captain into the sea to drown.

After he'd captured the ship, Fly and his rebels made a Jolly Roger flag, and changed the name of the ship to *Fame's Revenge*. The rebels decided to make William Fly their captain. They sold the slaves, then sailed to the coast of North Carolina. They captured five ships in a couple of months and the Carolina traders were terrified.

Fly had a terrible temper and if his enemies upset him he would have them whipped a hundred times. His pirate life didn't make him rich – he robbed ships of tobacco and cloth, logs or spices.

Captain Fly had captured Captain Atkinson of a trading ship and forced him to slave as a member of his crew. Atkinson was a good crew member but he was really waiting for his chance to rebel. It came when they attacked a schooner and Fly's most trusted men went off on a boarding party.

Atkinson and his captured comrades turned the tables on Fly and took him prisoner. They sailed him off to prison. Fly had only been a pirate for two months.

TERRY DEARY'S
PIRATE TALES

The Pirate Lord

Illustrated by Helen Flook

A & C BLACK
AN IMPRINT OF BLOOMSBURY
LONDON NEW DELHI NEW YORK SYDNEY

Chapter One
Mists and Mutton

Devon, 1587

Sit by the fire. Go on, you look as wet as a herring. When the mist rolls in off the sea, it goes through you like there's ice in your blood. Sit down. I'll fetch you a pot of my best ale.

There you are, sir, you should warm through in no time. The maid will light a fire in your bedroom and it'll be like toast when you're ready to go up.

Yes, I'm the landlord of this tavern. I own it. It's the finest tavern in Cornwall and I sell the finest ale. The name's Tom, sir, Tom Pennock.

I know what you're thinking. How does a rough fellow like me come to own a tavern as fine as The Golden Hind? I'll get the maid to fetch you a bowl of the best lamb stew you ever tasted... not mutton, mind you ... real lamb. And if you've a half hour to spare before bed, I'll tell you how I earned my money.

I made it at sea, sir. And, no, I wasn't a pirate... well, not really. If I *was* a pirate, then so was the greatest man that ever sailed the seven seas.

You'll have heard of Francis Drake... *Sir* Francis Drake they call him now. But I knew him back in 1577 when he was just plain Captain Drake to us.

I was ten years old when I first saw him. I was a skinny little lad, no higher than the rail on a poop deck. But I ate too much.

"That lad eats too much," my father said. "He'll ruin us. Bread for breakfast, cheese for dinner and cheese for supper. Eat, eat, eat, that's all he ever does. He'll have to go!"

7

"Go, Father?" I said. "Go where?"

"To a master – you work and he feeds you. Then your mother and me will be able to feed ourselves. A couple of your sisters are already serving in great houses. It's time for you to go, my lad."

"I could work with an ostler, Father, looking after horses. I like horses."

"Ha!" my father jeered. "You'd end up eating them. No, there's a ship in town. The men at the inn said the captain's looking for crew."

That was the only time my mother ever spoke up for me. "If you spent less time in that inn, Father, drinking away our money, you'd have more to feed our little Tom."

Father just snorted. "He'll have to get a job some time. The sooner he starts, the sooner he'll make his fortune."

"Fortune, Father?" I asked. "Can a sailor make a fortune?"

"Any man can make a fortune if he puts his mind to it."

"So why haven't *you* made a fortune, Father?" I asked.

"Shut up, son, and get your sea-boots on. You're off to see the sea."

He laughed at his joke.

I didn't.

Chapter Two
Gold and Goodbyes

I cried. I'm not ashamed to tell you, sir, I cried like a baby. I stood on the deck of the ship, the *Pelican*, and I sniffled.

Men and boys lined up on the sun-warmed planks. Some joked, some chatted like magpies and some stood grim-faced and angry. I was the only one weeping.

Suddenly, a cabin door opened and I had my first sight of Francis Drake. He wasn't a tall man, but he strutted around like our backyard bantam cock, eyes fierce in a wind-burned face, chest puffed out and beard ruffled by the breeze. Everyone fell silent.

The captain walked along the line, greeting some men as old friends. "Welcome on board, Jed Trickett... I see you're back for another shot at the Spanish, George Archer? Ah, Edward Marston... troublemaker, shirker and drunkard. Get off my ship!"

The man called Marston cursed Drake, spat on the deck and rambled back along the gangplank. He was halfway across when he lurched to the left and fell into Plymouth harbour. Everyone laughed and even I dried my tears and smiled.

Captain Drake reached me and asked, "Who have we here?"

My father jabbed me with his finger.

"Tom Pennock... sir," I said.

"And you want to serve our Queen Elizabeth, do you, Tom?"

I didn't know what he meant. Father spoke up. "He's the hardest-working lad you'll ever meet, Captain. Take our Tom with you and he'll kill twenty Spaniards before breakfast then swab the decks to clean up their blood."

Drake laughed. "Then he's the lad for me. I'll set you to work as a cabin boy – serving in the galley... you know what a galley is?"

"No, sir."

"It's the kitchen where we cook the ship's food... and when we go into battle, you'll be a powder monkey," Drake explained.

"He's a monkey all right," Father laughed.

"A powder monkey fetches gunpowder from the store below deck for the gunners. It's hot work and you have to be fast on your feet. Think you can do it?"

I had no idea if I could do it or not, but I said, "Yes, sir." I already knew I'd have walked into the mouth of a cannon for that great captain.

Drake nodded at my father. "He'll do. Take a golden sovereign from the ship's purser on the foredeck."

Father grinned and almost ran to the man with a chest of treasure. He hardly stopped to wave goodbye.

And that's how I came to serve with Captain Francis Drake. I was sold by my father for a piece of gold.

Chapter Three
Riches and Robin

For weeks we saw nothing but sea. I found I was one of the lucky ones. As Drake's little fleet of ships ploughed across the Atlantic Ocean, I was never sick. Bit by bit, I learned my job and I learned what our voyage was all about – treasure.

After I served the evening meal, the men sat below deck to eat it.

"The Spanish found gold and silver in South America," Jed Trickett told me. "They have an army of men out there working in the mines. They dig out tons of the stuff."

"They must be rich," I said.

"Well, the King of Spain is rich. The mine work is hard, and hotter than Hell, they say. A lot of men die."

"Are we going to dig in the mines?" I gasped. "I don't want to die!"

"No, Tom lad. The Spanish won't let us anywhere near their land. Our Queen Elizabeth has a much better idea. She waits till the Spanish dig out the gold and load it onto their galleons. Then she sends Captain Drake to rob the Spanish ships."

"And *that's* how we get rich?" I asked.

Trickett nodded. "Half the treasure goes to our queen and the sailors share the rest with Captain Drake."

I thought about this for a while. "So we're robbers? Pirates?" I asked. I was worried. Every Sunday, the priest warned us about stealing. God would punish us, he said.

Trickett laughed. "No, lad. We're privateers – in private business. Where do you think the Spanish get their gold?"

"From the mines?"

"They *steal* it, Tom. South America isn't their land. They make the natives into slaves. They force them to dig for the gold.

Then they send it back to Spain. We just punish the Spanish for being so wicked."

And I believed him. When he put it like that. I grinned. "We're like Robin Hood?"

"Exactly like Robin Hood, if Robin Hood had a ship."

We weren't pirates, we were Robin Hood's merry men. But there wasn't much to be merry about on that voyage.

Chapter Four
Storms and Skulls

Before we reached South America, we lost a lot of men. Some were washed overboard in storms, or crushed when a mast fell on the deck. Some killed each other in fights, and one man was executed for trying to start a mutiny against Captain Drake. But most of them died of sickness.

So many men died, we didn't have enough to crew all the ships. We sank two of the fleet in the Atlantic and just three vessels sailed on.

After two months, we landed for supplies in the place the Spanish call the Land of

Silver – 'Argentina' in their language.

We went ashore to gather fruit that would keep away sickness, and fresh water.

"I can't see any silver," I told Jed Trickett. I looked across the bleak beach and all I could find were bones. Scattered skulls had been pecked clean by rats and seabirds.

Captain Drake walked beside me and picked up a skull. "A sailor called Magellan came this way a hundred years ago," he told me. "Some of his men refused to go on, so he had them executed."

"Why did they refuse?"

Drake stroked his beard, which was longer and wilder than it had been when we left Plymouth. "Because they knew what was coming." He leaned forward and glared at me. "We've seen storms in the Atlantic, lad, but they're nothing to what we face next. When we sail around the southern tip of America, the seas are taller than three ships. Bad sailors get their ships snapped like dry twigs."

I trembled. "But we're not bad sailors, Captain Drake."

"We'll soon find out," he snorted. "Are you scared?"

"Yes."

"Then we'll leave you here with the skeletons," he said and walked back to the supply boat.

I ran after him.

The seas were as rough as the captain promised. No one slept for three days as we fought to keep the ship heading into the waves. If we let the waves hit us on the side, we'd be broken into splinters.

Every day, someone seemed to go missing. Waves like mountains washed over the deck and anyone caught in the open was carried away with them.

Men worked with buckets to keep the *Pelican* afloat. I took them bread and cheese, but it was wet and salty by the time they pushed it into their mouths. They looked as ghastly as the skeletons on the beach in Argentina.

I huddled in the corner of the galley, exhausted, and waited to die.

Chapter Five
Salt and Sun

Jed Trickett shook me till I woke. His face was crusted with dry salt, his lips were cracked and bleeding, and I thought he was a ghost come to take me to heaven. The ship was rocking but no longer being tossed up and down like a child's rag ball.

"We're through the worst," Jed said.

"I'm not dead?" I asked.

"I don't think so," he chuckled. "Come on deck and look at the Pacific Ocean. Not many English people have done that."

The sun dazzled me as it glinted off the clear water. A few weary men hauled on ropes to raise the sails. We were alone.

"Where are the other ships?" I asked.

"Gone, lad, gone," Drake said. He looked as tired as any man and his eyes were hollow caves. "One went down in the night... we couldn't save a single soul. The other was too battered to go on. I sent her back to England."

"But we got through," Jed said with a sigh. "The *Pelican's* a lucky ship."

Drake nodded. "And I've decided to change her name – from now on we'll call her the *Golden Hind*."

"*Golden Hind*?" I said. I liked the name. "So do we have to sail the *Golden Hind* through all that again, Captain?" I asked. "Are we going to get back home the way we came?"

"No. The world is like a ball, you know. If we keep sailing west, we'll end up where we started."

"Is that where we're headed now?"

Drake managed a grin. "Not till we've done what we came to do."

"Rob the Spanish," Jed Trickett said and rubbed his hands.

Drake turned on him. "Eat some fruit, Trickett... those cracked lips tell me you're going down with scurvy. If you get any worse, you'll be too dead to enjoy it."

Jed nodded and headed for the galley where the ship's cook was trying to boil up some dried beef into a stew.

Captain Drake looked to the stern of the ship. "Steersman, head north. There are some Spaniards who can't wait to give us their gold."

The men gave a cheer. It was a weak, croaking cheer, but the storms had failed to crush the hope from our hearts.

Chapter Six
Pacific Plots

It took us a month to reach the place that had the greatest treasure. We stopped along the way and raided small Spanish ports. Drake collected better maps from them, but when we raided Mocha Island, all he got was a nasty wound from the natives.

I stayed on the ship when the crew went on the raids. I remember the day they carried Captain Drake back onto the ship with his cheek sliced open. George Archer sewed it up with sail thread, and the captain was back in charge the next day. He always carried the scar after that.

As we sailed north on the *Golden Hind*, Drake placed a finger on the map. "That's where we're headed for, lads. Valparaiso. The biggest Spanish port on this coast. And that means the biggest ships with the biggest haul of treasure."

We reached Valparaiso harbour three days later. A galleon was sitting at anchor in the harbour. Drake called his men onto the deck. "That's a Spanish treasure ship," he said. "Would anyone care to make himself a little richer?"

We laughed. Our mood was better already. Drake sent me up to the top of the mast to get a better look. "She only has a handful of men to guard her," I called down.

"Let's knock her masts down with shot so she can't escape," Jed said.

Drake stroked his beard and thought for a while. Finally, he said, "Trickett."

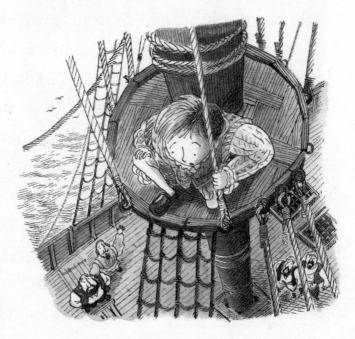

"Yes, sir?"

"If you were a guard on that Spanish ship, what would you do if this ship came at you firing all guns?"

"Fire back, sir."

"And if she fires back with those huge cannon, what might happen to your head if it was hit by a cannon ball?"

"It would bounce off!" someone called.

"Ah, but it might bounce onto the deck and smash the *Golden Hind*," Drake said. "Now, what would those Spanish think if we sailed close to her, said 'Hello' – in Spanish – and asked them to get some wine ready for us?"

The men looked uncertain.

Jed said, "They won't be expecting an English ship, that's for sure. The English have never sailed the Pacific, have they?"

It was a wild, mad plan that would never

work, I decided. But Drake's eyes were glowing with excitement. That's when he turned to me and said, "It's time we brought young Tom along on a raid. When they see a little cabin boy, they'll never guess we plan to rob them. Are you ready to make your fortune, Tom?" he asked.

No! my heart screamed. But "yes" was the word that came out of my mouth.

Chapter Seven
Ladders and Lanterns

The plan was formed quickly and by the time we reached the Spanish galleon, we all knew our parts.

The galleon looked like a floating castle. Black cannon gaped at us open-mouthed, ready to spit death at our small ship.

Jed Trickett led the way. "*Buenas tardes, encantado*," he called up the steep sides of the ship. "*Qué tal?*"

George Archer whispered to me. "That means, 'Hello, how are you?'" he explained.

The Spanish sailors lowered a rope ladder and Jed climbed up it. He jumped aboard the galleon and about ten of us followed him.

"*Amigo*!" the Spanish guard cried and opened his arms wide to greet Jed Trickett.

Jed Trickett punched him suddenly in the face. The man hit the deck with a clatter of his helmet. Our crew drew pistols and waved them. The Spanish guards turned, dived over the side and swam for the port.

No one tried to stop us as we searched the ship. I was the one who took a lantern down the narrow stairways. I was the powder monkey, quick and small enough to run below deck.

But the ship was like the maze old King Henry had made at Hampton Court Palace. I was soon lost and started to climb the ladders that led back up to the main deck. I ran back to where our crew waited. "Nothing," I said.

Jed looked over to the harbour, where the first escaping Spaniards were struggling onto the sea wall. "We have to be quick. They'll be back with muskets and gunships."

"We can sink them with their own cannon," I argued.

"There aren't enough of us to load and fire two cannon, even if we knew where they kept their powder and shot."

Suddenly, Drake hauled himself over the side of the ship. He stalked over to the groaning sailor who'd been knocked flat by Jed. "So, *amigo*. Where is the gold? Where is the treasure?"

The man looked up at Drake's scarred face and wild beard. "*Draco!*" he gasped.

That's what the Spanish call Drake, sir, *Draco*... it means Dragon.

"That's right... *Draco*," he replied. "Come on your ship breathing fire. Now, tell me where you store the treasure. *El oro?*"

I could see now that the guard wasn't much older than me. He stumbled to his feet. "*Draco* is devil. I no give my king *oro* to devil!" he cried.

"Let's hang him from the mast," Captain Drake said wearily. "Pass me that rope."

"No, that's cruel!" I shouted. "He's too young to die."

Drake turned his dark eyes on me. "No one is too young to die. Not even you, Tom lad. If you want to argue with your captain, that is mutiny. And you know what happens to men who mutiny?"

"They get killed," I said.

"So? Do you want to hang alongside your Spanish friend? Or do you want me to cut off your head with my rusty old sword?"

Chapter Eight
Noose and Neck

I tell you, sir, I've faced a hundred freezing storms and laughed at them. But those words from Captain Drake turned me colder than an albatross's foot.

I don't remember what I said. "Don't cut off my head, sir... and don't hang me... I didn't mean to argue, oh, spare me, sir..."

Drake turned his back on my bubbling and babbling. "Put a rope around the Spanish lad's neck," he ordered.

Jed hurried to obey. The Spanish boy's olive skin turned pale green with terror as a noose slipped over his neck.

Captain Drake jerked on the end of the rope. "The gold... *oro*... where is the *oro*, lad?"

The boy just shook his head.

Drake shrugged and dragged the Spaniard up the stairs onto the rear deck. It was a drop of six foot onto the main deck. He threw one end of the rope over the spar of the mizzenmast. "*Oro*... or die... *quieres morir?*" the captain asked as he pushed the boy towards the rail. He picked him up and sat him on the rail till the Spaniard looked at the drop below him.

I looked at the end of the rope. Captain Drake hadn't tied it to anything. The boy didn't know that.

"*Oro?*" Drake asked.

The boy's mouth moved, but no words came out. Drake pushed him. The boy dropped the six feet to the deck and

44

screamed. But the rope didn't stop him. He tumbled to the deck a sobbing, twitching jellyfish.

Drake walked slowly down the steps to where he lay. "*Oro?*"

"*En la parte trasera.*"

Drake nodded. "At the stern of the galleon, lads. We've been looking in the wrong place. Find it, Tom," he ordered.

I ran past the blubbering boy and through the ship's cabins. I was the one who found the twenty crates. They were too heavy to move and were bound with leather and iron so they were too strong to open.

Jed Trickett brought tools from the *Golden Hind* and after long minutes sweating in the stinking dark, we managed to open one.

Even in the weak light of the lanterns, the gold and silver bars were dazzling. No one was able to take his eyes off the magical metal. When Jed Trickett finally spoke it was in a whisper. "Let's get it back on the *Golden Hind*," he said.

As we hauled the first bucket up on deck, George Archer cried, "Spanish soldiers! The Spanish are sending their gunboats out from harbour. If we don't move soon, we'll be dead meat."

Chapter Nine
Boats and Bullets

Drake gave his orders quickly and calmly. "The Spanish are coming from Valparaiso to the east. We'll unload to the west so the galleon shelters us. Jed Trickett... you hold them off."

Jed snorted. "By myself, Captain?"

"No, young Tom here will help you."

"Me?"

"Yes, you, Tom lad. Are you arguing again?"

"No, Captain," I said quickly.

"Take two muskets, powder and shot. Trickett will fire a musket while you load the other one. That'll give them something to think about. Now move, before I throw you to the fishes," he said.

We moved. We looked through one of the cannon ports and saw three gunboats heading towards us with about thirty soldiers in each. They were heading into the west wind, so they needed to be rowed by clumsy oarsmen. The boats were slow, but they would reach us before a quarter hour was gone.

Jed took the first musket and fired a shot that splashed harmlessly into the sea. "Missed," he muttered as I took the musket and passed him a loaded one.

Moments later twenty musket balls splintered the wood beside us. "They're good shots!" Jed laughed. "Better than me."

"The next round of shots could hit me!" I squawked.

Jed nodded. "That's one good reason for moving to another gun port," he said and crawled quickly along the deck to where another black cannon stood. "If I fire from here, they'll think we have quite a few musketeers... that'll slow them down."

I ran after him, keeping my head below the wooden rail.

Captain Drake was helping his men unload the treasure onto the boat. He watched it sail across to the *Golden Hind* and unload while our crew brought more onto the deck of the galleon.

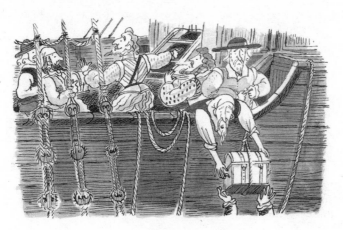

"How are we doing, Trickett?" he asked.

"Keeping them guessing," he replied.

Drake shook his head. "This is too slow," he sighed. He called across the water with waving arms. "Bring the *Golden Hind* alongside – we'll load straight onto her."

Another round of musket fire smashed into the side of the ship. "I've been hit," Jed Trickett moaned, and fell backwards with blood streaming down his face.

The captain ran across to the deck. I thought he was going to help patch Jed's wound, but he didn't. No, that wasn't Drake's way. Instead, he pulled the wounded man away from the side and snatched up the musket. "It's you and me now, Tom, against the might of Spain. Keep loading."

"Yes, sir," I said.

As my captain kept firing, I saw the Spanish boy begin to slip across the deck towards us. I'd just loaded a musket, and I pointed it at him. I'd never fired a gun in my young life, but I'd have shot him if he'd tried to harm my captain.

The boy shook his head and pointed at Jed, who was groaning and clutching at his face. "*Ayudará*," he said.

"*Ayud*... aid... aid him?"

The boy nodded. He tore at his shirt sleeve and made a bandage to stop the bleeding. If you ask me, he saved my friend's life.

But I was too busy loading muskets to worry about Jed just then. The Spanish gunboats were drawing nearer – the oarsmen clattering into the soldiers, who were standing up and trying to fire at us. I felt a shudder as the *Golden Hind* nudged into us. Loading the gold went much quicker. Our crew tipped the buckets down onto the *Golden Hind*, which was much smaller than the galleon.

At last the gunboats drew close enough for the Spanish to haul out their small cannon. Captain Drake and I watched as they loaded a stone cannonball and raised the barrel towards us.

Drake snorted. "They won't fire on one of their own galleons."

Three things happened very quickly. There was a puff of smoke and the stone ball flew towards us. The rail near our heads shattered into a thousand pieces. And, strangest of all, their cannon crashed backwards in the gunboat and sent Spanish soldiers tumbling, screaming into the water. The kick from the gun was so great it cracked the hull and we could see the gunboat start to fill with water. Soldiers scrambled to reach the other two gunboats, grabbed for the oars and almost upset them.

Drake laughed, rose to his feet and took off his hat. He waved it at the panicking Spanish. "*Adios, amigos...* from *Draco*!" he cried.

Then, to me, he said, "Time to go home, Tom lad."

Chapter Ten
Wealth and Wounds

We helped Jed down onto the *Golden Hind* and sailed off into the western sunset.

Captain Drake stood at the tiller that evening and said to me, "How does it feel to be a pirate, Tom Pennock?"

"Oh, but Captain Drake, I'm not! I'm a good citizen of England. I'm not a pirate."

"You are now, Tom," he said quietly. "You are now."

You know the rest, sir. We sailed on robbing more Spanish ships of their gold and silver, spices and jewels. Then headed west across the Pacific, past India and Africa, and home at last with a ship almost sinking with treasure.

The queen's share of the treasure was more than all the taxes she gathered that year. Captain Drake was a hero. Queen Elizabeth came aboard the *Golden Hind* in London and made him *Sir* Francis.

The queen was rich. But what about the English sailors? There were just 59 of us came home safe. We shared a quarter of the treasure 59 ways. More money than most men see in a lifetime.

But I'd had enough of the sea. I'd made so many friends and then lost them in the southern storms. All the money in Spain wouldn't bring my drowned friends back again. Jed Trickett knew how I felt. He said he wanted to buy an inn and settle down. I gave him my share of the treasure and between us we bought this place.

So how do I come to own it now, sir? Ah, that wound on poor Jed's face never healed. Not really. He was always sickly after our raid on Valparaiso.

No sooner had we opened the inn, and changed its name to The Golden Hind, than Jed died. He had no wife or family.

The inn was all mine.

And that's the end of the story. I hope you enjoyed your lamb stew, sir. It's been good serving you. Yes, I enjoy my life as a landlord. It's better than being a pirate, sir.

When I was a pirate I was one of the 59 lucky ones. But you have to pay for your treasures, sir. And a pirate pays in blood.

Aye, in blood.

Epilogue

In the story Tom Pennock and Jed Trickett are made up. But the tale of Francis Drake and his famous voyage around the world is true enough.

He set off in November 1577. Only the *Pelican* made the trip through the storms at the southern tip of South America. After that, Drake changed her name to the *Golden Hind*.

His crew really did raid the port of Valparaiso using a trick – pretending to be friendly Spanish sailors.

And he really did scare a Spanish sailor into revealing the location of the loot by pretending to hang him.

At the end of his two-year voyage, Captain Drake returned home in September 1580 to be made a knight – Sir Francis Drake.

Queen Elizabeth took half of all the treasure that Drake and his men had fought and died for. Her share was greater than all the taxes she collected in England in a year. She wanted more and sent off new fleets of pirates to rob the Spanish. None of them came back with as much treasure as Drake's Pacific voyage.

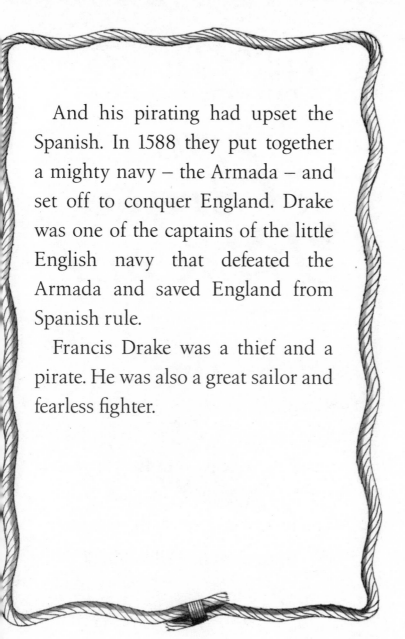

And his pirating had upset the Spanish. In 1588 they put together a mighty navy – the Armada – and set off to conquer England. Drake was one of the captains of the little English navy that defeated the Armada and saved England from Spanish rule.

Francis Drake was a thief and a pirate. He was also a great sailor and fearless fighter.

TERRY DEARY'S
PIRATE TALES

The Pirate Prisoner

Illustrated by Helen Flook

A & C BLACK
AN IMPRINT OF BLOOMSBURY
LONDON NEW DELHI NEW YORK SYDNEY

Chapter One
Sand and Slave

Nevis Island, Caribbean, 1680

It was hot. The sun burned down on Nevis Island and made steam rise up from the forests. The girl ran along the yellow-grey sands, her thin dress flapping round her skinny legs.

"I'm going to be late," she panted. "I mustn't be late." Her dark brown skin was shining with sweat. "I have to save him. Have to. Have to."

She reached the edge of the small town and raced along the dusty streets, past the poor wooden shacks...

past the fine wooden houses of the rich folk... and up to the great stone building in the centre.

A soldier stood guard at the great doors. He swatted flies that buzzed around his head. "Can I go in?" the girl begged.

"I'm not stopping you," the soldier said with a shrug.

"Has the trial started?" she asked.

The man just shrugged again. "How would I know?"

"Because you're on guard. You're here to stop people getting in," she said, crossly.

"No, I'm not. I'm here to stop the wicked ones escaping."

"Wicked ones like the pirate?"

"Men like the pirate."

"Don't let him escape, Sergeant... erm..."

"Private. Private Simpson."

"Pleased to meet you, Private Simpson. I'm Louisiana Le Moyne."

"Big name for a little lady."

"You can call me Lou. Everybody else does."

The man leaned forward. "I'm not sure I want to call you anything. I don't have to speak to a slave girl."

Lou smiled brightly. "Then I'll just go in," she told him.

"Then you just do that," said Private Simpson.

Lou entered the cool shade of the stone courthouse, through the heavy oak doors and into the courtroom itself. She was just in time to see the people rise lazily to their feet as the judge walked in.

"All rise for Judge Jenkins," a clerk cried a little late.

Lou slipped into a seat at the back and watched a grey-haired white man in black robes sit in the judge's chair. An Englishman, she decided.

Judge Jenkins shuffled some parchment in front of him. He looked across at the wooden box where a red-haired, wild-eyed man glared back.

"Are you Jack Greaves?"

About fifty people had crowded into the room to watch. They turned their eyes towards the prisoner. They waited for him to say, "I am."

Instead, he bellowed, "Who wants to know? Eh? What business is it of yours?"

Chapter Two
Sugar and Scot

Judge Jenkins blinked and his pale lips went tight with fury. "This may be the island of Nevis, but it is an English court of law. You will behave as if you are in England," he said quietly.

"I'm not English. I'm Scottish, just as my parents were Scottish, and I don't like you English."

The judge sighed. "If you're going to be foolish, I'll have you taken off to the cells and we'll have the trial without you."

"Pah," Greaves snorted and looked out through the high windows to the clear sky as if he didn't care.

"Are you the pirate known as Red-legs Greaves?" the judge asked.

"I'm a sugar farmer. I have twenty slaves and they're waiting for me back on my farm. If you lock me away, they won't know what to do. They'll starve."

"We will," Lou moaned softly.

"Before you were a sugar farmer, you were a pirate," the judge said slowly.

"Who says?" the Scotsman asked.

"I do," a man called out.

Lou turned and saw a large man in a fine blue suit with an expensive linen shirt.

The judge smiled. "Master Ellis!" he said in a voice as soft as a dove. "Step forward."

The rich man stood in front of the judge. "Ten years ago, I was sailing on one of my ships with a load of spice."

"And what happened, Master Ellis?"

Ellis turned, stretched out an arm and pointed at Greaves. "Red-legs Greaves there stopped my ship. He robbed me and left me penniless."

"Penniless?" Greaves roared. "Penniless? In a suit that cost more than a dozen slaves? You're a lying English toad, Ellis."

"Silence," the judge snapped. He turned to Master Ellis again and asked, "Tell me, why do you call him Dead-legs?"

"Red-legs, your honour. He's from Scotland. They wear kilts up there. Here in the Indies, their pale knees turn red. All the pirates called him Red-legs."

"And you saw his red legs when he robbed you?"

"I did, your honour."

The judge nodded. He pulled a square of black cloth from under his table. He placed it on his head. "Jack Red-legs Greaves, I sentence you to hang in chains. Tomorrow morning. May God have mercy on your soul."

"No!" Lou cried. "You can't do that to my master!"

Chapter Three
Silence and Cells

"Silence in court," the judge said.

"But what will the slaves do without him?" Lou cried.

"The estate will belong to the court...
and we will sell it. You will have a new
master," the judge said.

"I'll buy it," Master Ellis said.

"Good man," the judge said, smiling.
"It's probably worth a thousand pounds."

"I'll give you five hundred... cash,"
Ellis said.

Judge Jenkins nodded. "You can pay
me later."

"But Master Greaves is a wonderful master," Lou argued. "He's the kindest slave owner on the whole of Nevis Island. Everybody says so."

"Silence in court."

"Master Ellis is a monster – he beats and whips and starves his slaves," the girl went on.

"Only the lazy ones," Ellis sneered. "And the cheeky ones. There is a whip in my house just waiting for you when I take over."

"Master Greaves is right – you're a toad. A fat, slimy toad," Lou wailed.

"Silence in court, girl, or I'll whip you myself," the judge shouted.

"It isn't fair," Lou sobbed.

"That's enough. Your master will spend the night in the dungeon below the courthouse. He will hang in chains at sunrise. And *you*, girl, will spend the night with him. That will teach you to hold your evil little tongue. Private... take them both down to the cells."

Red-legs Greaves shook his head. "Oh, Lou, you foolish child. What have you done?"

"Spoken up for you, Master Greaves," she said, as she was pushed down the gloomy stairs toward the prison cell. "I thought the

English were famous for being fair. Well, they're not. You haven't been a pirate for years."

They entered the filthy cell and the door closed behind them with a boom like the sound of doom. Red-legs Greaves walked to the small window and looked out through the bars. "I've had a lucky life. When it ends tomorrow, I won't complain."

Lou didn't answer.

The tears she sniffed back were making her throat too tight to speak.

Chapter Four
Cromwell and Killing

Red-legs Greaves scraped green scum off the water bucket in the corner and scooped it over his ruddy face. "I'm sorry to leave you like this," he sighed.

"You've been such a good master," Lou whimpered.

The Scot nodded. "Aye. That's because I know what it's like to be a slave. I was born into slavery."

Lou looked up, wide-eyed. "You? A slave? But you're a white man."

He shrugged. "Back in Britain there was a man called Oliver Cromwell. He cut off the head of King Charles and then he captured all the king's friends. My mother and father fought for the king. When they lost, Cromwell sold them as slaves and had them sent to Barbados. That's where I was born. A slave."

"But how did you become a pirate?" the girl asked.

"My parents died... the heat and the diseases did for them. I was sold to a master who enjoyed beating me. So one night I decided to escape. There was just one way off the island – "

"A boat?"

Red-legs laughed. "Aye. I swam across Carlisle Bay to the main harbour in Bridgetown. About two miles. Then I hid on board a ship so I could sail away and make my fortune."

"And did you?"

"Lord, no, lassie. How was I to know it was a pirate ship I was hiding on? The captain was the wicked Captain Hawkins."

"Wicked?"

"Aye. He wasn't happy robbing traders. He had to torture the captured crews for fun and then he killed them – even the women. When he found me, he said I had to work for him, or die."

"So you became a pirate for Captain Hawkins," Lou said. "But if you killed all the people you robbed... how is Master Ellis still alive? If you'd killed him, he wouldn't be there in court."

Red-legs Greaves held up his hands. "No, young Lou. I said Captain Hawkins was a ruthless, killing pirate. But *I* only ever killed one man. And that was the best day's work I ever did."

Lou's mouth fell open. "Oh, Master Greaves, who did you kill?"

"Ah, young Lou, that comes later in my story. You'll have to wait and see…"

Chapter Five
Bars and Bread

As the sun sank lower in the sky, it grew a little cooler in the cell. Red-legs Greaves stood at the bars of the cell and looked out. Lou was too short to see over the windowsill.

The iron bars were as rusty and red as Master Greaves' legs. The man tugged at them. They rattled, but all his strength couldn't pull them out.

A guard brought them a bottle of wine, some fresh water and a plate of bread and ham. "Wine? Ham? A fine meal for a poor prisoner!" the Scot cried.

The guard shuffled his feet and looked at the floor. "We always give a good meal to the men we're going to hang."

"Ah! You send them to Hell with a full belly?" Red-legs said, and laughed.

Lou groaned. "You aren't going to Hell, Master Greaves. You were the kindest master on the island. Everybody said that."

"But I killed a man, remember."

"Who was it?"

The Scot poured a little wine into the cup and added water. He gave it to Lou. "I spent a year on Hawkins' ship," he said. "I soon found that all the crew hated him. They hated his cruel ways. He was even cruel to his own men. If anyone crossed him, he had them marooned."

"What's that?"

"A marooned man is set down on a desert island with a little food and a pistol. If he's lucky, he may shoot something, like a goat, and eat a little. But when the powder and the bullets run out, he'll slowly starve to death. It's something all pirates are afraid of."

Lou shook her head. "But if you hated him so much, why didn't you all get together and maroon *him*?" Lou asked.

"Two reasons. Captain Hawkins was a powerful man and no one had the courage to fight him. And he was a *good* pirate. He led us to many rich ships, stole a lot of treasure and made us all a fortune."

"Like Master Ellis," Lou said sadly. "The cruel and the wicked get rich."

Red-legs nodded slowly as he chewed on a piece of ham. "But, like me, even the rich can't buy their life. Not when it's time to die."

"Captain Hawkins died?"

"He did."

"How? Tell me!" Lou cried.

The Scot tasted the ham as if it were the last meal he'd ever eat. He smacked his lips, sipped a little wine and ran a hand over his mouth. "Captain Hawkins met a man who was foolish enough to fight him."

"Who?" Lou asked softly.

"Me," Red-legs Greaves replied.

Chapter Six
Swords and Sunset

"We saw a French spice ship just off the island of Saint Kitts," Red-legs Greaves explained. "She was a fast ship and it took us all day to catch her. That upset Captain Hawkins. By the time we came alongside the Frenchie, his blood was boiling with rage. He gave us the order to kill everyone."

"You couldn't do that," Lou said.

"They were simple sailors, with no guns and no swords. Just the knives they used to eat their food. 'I'm not doing it,' I told Hawkins. 'There's no need to kill the crew. Let's just take their spice and sell it in

Bridgetown. No one has to get hurt!'"

"Was he angry?" Lou asked.

"I think Captain Hawkins was too *shocked* to be angry. No one ever argued with him. He just stared at me. Then he said, 'How many sailors are there on that French ship, Greaves?' I looked across the sea and said, 'Twenty.' And he drew his cutlass and said, 'There are twenty-one men going to die today. You are number one.' Then he rushed at me with his sword raised in the air."

"But you drew your sword?" Lou asked.

"I never carried a sword. I was a sailor – I mended the sails and steered the ship, I scrubbed the decks and loaded supplies. I wasn't a fighter."

"But you beat Captain Hawkins?"

"He rushed at me. His arm was raised high in the air. He thought I would run away. Instead, I ran towards him. I grabbed his sword arm. And twisted it. He was a strong man, but his fine leather boots skidded on the deck and he fell... on his sword. I still hear his cry in my nightmares. He dropped to his knees. His eyes grew cloudy. He tried to pluck the sword from his side, but his hands were shaking too much."

"And he died," Lou said.

Red-legs shook his head. "The next thing I remember, the crew were cheering.

They threw Hawkins' body over the side and raised me up on their shoulders. Then they told me I was their new captain."

"So that's how you became a pirate," Lou said. "I bet you were a *good* pirate."

The sun had now set and clouds over Nevis Peak blotted out the stars. In the perfect darkness, Red-legs said, "A pirate is a pirate. And a captured pirate is a dead pirate. Wake me when the sky grows light. I want to see my last sunrise."

Minutes later, the old pirate was snoring softly while the young slave girl quietly prayed.

"Hello, God. God? Are you there? Master Greaves used to be a pirate. But he's a good, kind man. Do you think you could do one of your miracles to get him free? Thank you, God."

Chapter Seven
Sunrise and Screams

Lou woke to see the clouds were a pearly grey colour. It was only an hour till sunrise. She shook the pirate gently. "Master Greaves. You wanted me to wake you before dawn."

The old man shook his head and splashed water over his face. "Thanks, lassie." He sat up and looked at her. "I wish there was something I could do for you. I know Master Ellis will treat you badly. That will be his revenge."

"Because you robbed him?"

"Aye. When I became a pirate captain, I set down new rules. We could jump on board a trading ship. We could push the crew aside – even tie them up – and steal their cargo. But none of my men must shed a drop of blood. The crew liked the new rules as much as they'd hated old Captain Hawkins."

"What did you do if they *did* hurt somebody?"

"We'd pay the man his share of the treasure we'd won... and put him ashore at the nearest port."

Lou's eyes shone with pride. "So you were a *kind* pirate?"

"I tried not to hurt anyone. Mind you, the victims still didn't like it. I remember robbing James Ellis' ship. When we went on board, he started firing pistols at the crew. He hit one lad in the leg, so we had to rush at him when he tried to reload. Then we tied him to the mast. The lad that was hit was upset. He went and pulled Ellis' pants down... and the ladies on the ship all laughed."

"That would make him angry," Lou said wisely.

"He was ranting about what he'd do to us. He said he'd see us all hang from the gallows... and now he's going to get his wish."

"But you gave up pirating years ago."

"We did well. We made a fortune... even the lowly deck scrubbers went home rich. I had enough money to buy a sugar farm here on Nevis Island and enough left over to buy a dozen slaves. That was fifteen years ago, before you were born. Yesterday, I went to the market, and Ellis spotted me. You know the rest."

Lou's eyes filled with tears. "I prayed for a miracle," she murmured.

The Scot ruffled her hair and laughed. "You're a good child. Maybe the rope will snap and I'll end up with a broken leg instead of a broken neck. Maybe that will be your miracle."

"How can you joke about it?" she gasped.

Somewhere above them, they heard a heavy door open. Footsteps clumped down the stairs. Keys rattled on the jailer's fist.

Lou backed up against the wall. The bucket of slimy water stood by her side. The smooth surface began to ripple. The bucket trembled. The timbers in the cell creaked.

There was a huge crash as stones fell from the roof and the walls of the courthouse crumbled. Through the bars of the window came a roar and the clear morning air was filled with the dust of a hundred tumbling buildings. Screams of the people mixed with the roar of falling stone.

Lou felt the solid cell wall at her back shaking. "What's happening?" she squeaked in terror.

Red-legs Greaves gave a thin smile. "Earthquake," he said.

Chapter Eight
Dust and Destruction

Lou huddled in a corner as the courthouse began to fall. Their cell below the ground cracked and dust filled the air till it was as dark as night again. There were more great shudders like the trembling body of a dying giant. Then, slowly, all fell silent.

Stones trickled through the twisted bars of the cell. Lou spat the thick dust from her mouth and coughed. "Master Greaves?"

"I'm here, child."

"Are you hurt?"

The man chuckled. "Takes more than a little earthquake to kill a Scot. In fact, they'll all be a bit too busy to hang me this morning. I've seen it before on these islands. It's the rich folk in their stone houses that suffer most."

Lou nodded. The dust was settling and she could see her master, red hair turned white with stone dust and ruddy face ghost-pale. "The slaves in the tar-paper shacks should be safe enough. Should I go and see?"

"There's a whole courthouse fallen on top of those stairs, lassie. You'll never get out that way," the man said gently.

"No," Lou told him. "But the bars have come away from the window. Look. I can squeeze through."

Red-legs Greaves walked across the cracked cell floor, ducking under the broken beams. He tugged at the row of bars and they fell with a clatter into the room. The dusty air outside was still. The way was open.

"Looks like your prayer was answered, lassie," the man said. "You go first and give a hand to pull me out."

A minute later, the two prisoners stood in the shattered street and looked around. People, bleeding and bruised, dazed and dying, lay amongst the ruins of the town. "Shall we help them?" Lou asked.

The man shook his head slowly. "The earthquake shakes the sea, too. In an hour or so, some huge waves could wash over the island. If we patch them up, we'll be saving them for the sea to drown."

"Will we drown, too?" the girl groaned.

"There are just two safe places – on top of Nevis Peak, or out at sea."

"Have we time to climb the mountain?" Lou asked.

"No, but we do have time to run to the harbour and take a ship. Come on, lassie, run! Run for your life!"

Chapter Nine
Luck and Louisiana

They ran. They ran through the torn town and down to the harbour where dazed sailors were wandering in wonder at the sight all around them.

"What about my friends, the other slaves?" Lou moaned.

"The estate is high enough up," Master Greaves panted as he hurried behind the girl. "They'll be safe. There'll be so few people left on the island, they'll be able to find their own freedom."

"Freedom," Lou repeated, and ran on.

The captain of a sugar ship stood on deck, as still and stiff as the main mast on his ship.

"Captain McKay!" Red-legs Greaves shouted. "Are you sailing with my sugar crop today?"

"I... I was going to... but... but..." the man burbled.

"Then cast off at once," the old pirate ordered.

"Yes, Master Greaves, but I don't have a full crew. Just two men stayed on board. We don't know where the rest are."

Red-legs grinned. "You have an old sea dog and a runaway slave to help. Now cast off before the great wave hits the island and wets my good sugar."

The captain stirred into life and shouted at his two sailors to make ready to leave. "Where to, Master Greaves?" one asked.

The old pirate wrapped an arm around the thin shoulders of the girl in the tattered dress. "Where to, Lou?"

"To freedom, Master Greaves... to freedom!"

When they reached the safety of another shore, their adventure was over. The sugar was sold and Red-legs Greaves used the money to buy a small sugar plantation on a distant island where no one knew him.

The plantation was popular with all the workers because Red-legs Greaves was such a good master. His manager was a young lady who called herself Miss Louisiana Le Moyne... though Greaves always called her simply Lou.

The years passed, and master and manager shared a table on the porch of the fine house he had built for them.

"You could be the richest man on the island, if you wanted," Lou told him as they looked out across the bay to the sea as green as emeralds. "And if you didn't give away so much to the poor."

"When you are as lucky as me, you need to share your luck around. I was a pirate once, and now I'm paying back my treasure to the people who need it the most."

Lou smiled. She knew he was right. "Though there are some things money can't buy, old master."

"Are there, young Lou? And what in the world might they be?"

"Miracles, master. Miracles."

And the old Scotsman didn't argue.

Epilogue

In the story, the girl Lou is not true, but the rest of the tale is.

Red-legs Greaves was a Scotsman, born into slavery, who escaped to become a pirate with the ruthless Captain Hawkins. He was forced to kill Hawkins when they finally fell out. He took over the pirate ship but he refused to kill or torture, and made sure his pirates harmed none of the men they fought.

Red-legs made a fortune with his raids and retired to start a sugar plantation on Nevis Island. But an angry victim of his piracy betrayed him and he was arrested. The judge said the Scotsman should hang, but the day before the execution an earthquake destroyed his prison. Many guards and prisoners were killed, but Red-legs managed to escape and enjoy his freedom again. It was a miracle.

He joined the crew of a whaling ship and served the captain well. He became a pirate-hunter and helped to capture a gang of pirates that had been ruining the whaling fleet.

The King of England gave Red-legs a pardon for his good work. The old pirate settled onto a new plantation, where he was loved for his kindness.

He died peacefully of old age... unlike most pirates of the time.

TERRY DEARY'S PIRATE TALES

The Pirate Queen

Illustrated by Helen Flook

A & C BLACK
AN IMPRINT OF BLOOMSBURY
LONDON NEW DELHI NEW YORK SYDNEY

Chapter One
Bald and Bold

Ireland, 1593

My ma was the greatest pirate that ever lived. My ma was the terror of the Irish Sea. My ma made strong men turn to water.

My ma was Grace O'Malley.

How do I know she was the greatest terror that ever turned water into pirates... I mean the greatest pirate that ever turned the Irish Sea into water... I mean... oh, you know what I mean.

How do I know she was great? Because she told me. She told me every day she was back home.

"Catherine," she said. "Catherine, your ma is the greatest pirate that ever lived."

"Are you really, Ma?" I asked and looked up at her fine figure with her cropped, red hair. Her hair was so short they called her Granuaile in the old Irish language. If you're not Irish, that means 'bald'. (If you *are* Irish, it still means 'bald'.)

Most girls are proud of their mothers and think they're as pretty as a shamrock in bloom. Now, even when I was too young to walk, I knew my ma wasn't a beauty. Her face was blotched by the salty west winds and scarred with fifty fights. Her nose was broken and one eye was half blind.

But I was still proud of my ma, Grace O'Malley. Of course I wanted to be just like her. I wanted to bring back riches to our castle in Connacht. If you're not Irish, then you need to know that Connacht is the grandest county in Ireland. (If you *are* Irish, it's still a grand county on the west coast of Ireland... and I don't care how grand you think *your* county might be, I'll fight anyone who says Connacht's not the best.)

As I say, I wanted to be just like my ma. I wanted to be a pirate. The problem was

I could not wait. And that's how I got into all that trouble.

Mind you, it was just as well I did cause that trouble, because it was me who saved the life of Grace O'Malley, Pirate Queen of Connacht.

I remember the night we sat in the great hall of the castle. The chill wind blew wild around Clare Island and all the shutters

in Ireland couldn't keep it out. Even the blazing log fire didn't warm the room very much. My ma and her captains sat close to the fire. The poor peasants and the children like me shivered in the draughty dim corners with the dogs.

The last crumb of bread was eaten and the last bit of mutton gristle spat on the floor and Grace O'Malley filled her wine cup. "Here's good luck to the pirates of Connacht!" she cried. "And may the seas be full of treasure ships tomorrow!"

The captains cheered and the sailors on the benches waved their hats. In the corners we coughed and sniffled.

"Tell us a story, Queen Grace!" a sailor shouted.

Of course she wasn't a real queen, just the leader of the O'Malley clan, but the pitiless pirates of Clare Island would follow her to the death. That's what mattered.

"A story?" she smiled. "I don't know any stories."

The men laughed. "Tell us about when you were a wee girl," old Hugh O'Neil called out.

11

"Aye!" the others cried. They settled down with their warm wine and turned to face their pirate queen.

And so she began...

Chapter Two
Sea and Swords

"When I was a girl," Grace said, "my mother wanted me to be a lady. She taught me sewing and mending, painting and playing the lute, curling my long red hair in ringlets and making perfume from rose petals. I was so *bored* I could have jumped off the top of Clare Castle tower!"

"Hurrah!" the pirates cheered.

"I begged my father to take me with him on his next trip to Spain, but he said he wouldn't dare... my mother would kill him!"

"Haaaa!" the pirates laughed.

"So I cut off my hair, stole clothes from a serving boy, and went down to the harbour. I walked over the gangplank to my father's galley and told a sailor I was the new cabin boy.

"I hid in a cabin till the ship was far out to sea and then I slipped away and found my father."

"Ooooh!" the pirates sighed, knowing what a fierce temper the old chief had.

"First he said he'd throw me over the side to feed the fishes. But I told him I was too skinny to feed a minnow. He laughed and said I could stay, but if he attacked another ship, I had to go below deck. And so I sailed to Spain with my father's fleet of four galleys."

"Hurrah!"

"One morning the lookout sighted an English cog and the crew raced to clear the decks. Father was too busy to notice me on the forecastle. That cog was as slow as a donkey in the water and we soon caught up with her, threw grappling lines across and made ready to climb aboard."

"Ooooh!"

"But what Father didn't know was the cog had a troop of English soldiers aboard, and instead of us jumping aboard them, *they* jumped onto our decks."

"Ahhhh!"

"Swords flashed and muskets blasted. I didn't want to be trapped in a cabin with no way out. So I climbed the rigging ropes that hung from the main mast and watched them fighting down below. Slowly, the English drove back our crew, and my father was facing an evil English soldier..."

"Down with the English," the pirates muttered.

"Then my father's sword snapped. He was helpless. The English soldier raised his weapon to split my father's skull in two. And that's when I jumped from the rigging, landed on the enemy's sword arm and saved my father's life.

"Father picked up the sword and gave a mighty scream. Aieeee! He led the men forward and drove the English into the sea."

"Hurrah!"

"And from that time on I was a member of the crew. And now I am your leader."

The men roared and drank and others stood up to tell their tales. But it was the *start* of Ma's story that *I* remembered. That's what kept me awake that night under my sheepskin cloak... not just the cold. And that's why I did what I did the next day...

Chapter Three
Rats and Ropes

The October dawn was damp and drizzly. Most dawns are on the west coast of Ireland. The men in our pirate crew hurried to their ships with heads down and backs loaded with food sacks and water barrels, weapons and tools.

The ship smelled of tar where the planks had been patched to keep the grey waters out. I stepped onto the shaking gangplank. Or maybe it was a steady gangplank and it was my *legs* that were shaking. No one tried to stop me. I darted into the cabin on the stern deck and waited in the dark with only a family of rats for company.

At last, I felt the ship begin to move and the old oak timbers creak as they twisted in the waves. Feet ran over the decks, ropes and pulleys cracked and clacked in the breeze, and men shouted to one another over the crash of the waves against the hull.

I rose stiffly and sent the rats scuttling into a hole in the cabin wall. I opened the door and cold spray hit me in the face like a slap with a wet fish. My ma was standing by the steering oar at the stern, looking at a yellowed chart and talking to the steersman.

"When we've passed Lands End, head east-north-east," she was saying.

I said, "Hello, Ma!" and waited to see her scarred face burst into a smile like sunshine. She turned. Her face was as grey as a thundercloud and twice as dangerous. "What are you doing here, you idiot child?" she screamed.

"Doing what *you* did, Ma! Going off to sea to be a pirate," I said. I tried to sound cheerful, but my voice was shaking.

"I'm not having you eating the food or drinking the water that my crew need. I'm not having you getting under our feet when we fight. I'm not having you bring bad luck to this voyage," she said sternly.

"I won't, Ma," I croaked and I felt tears bubbling behind my eyes.

Ma turned to a passing sailor. "Throw this child overboard."

"But, Ma —" I began to wail, as the man strode towards me. His hand touched my wet leather jerkin and I wriggled away.

I jumped down onto the main deck and headed for the mast. The crew stopped work to watch the fun as the pirate stalked after me.

Ropes hung down from the mainsail and I gripped one. I hauled myself up and felt the sailor's hand on my shoe. I pulled upwards and the shoe came away in his hand, but at least I was free.

I kept climbing till I reached a small platform – the crow's nest – at the top of the mast. In the wind it swayed like a willow tree. I clung on tight.

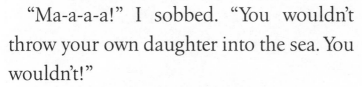

"You'll come down when you're cold or hungry enough," Ma snarled. "Or you'll fall asleep and drop into the sea."

"Ma-a-a-a!" I sobbed. "You wouldn't throw your own daughter into the sea. You wouldn't!"

I don't know if she really would. I'll never know. Maybe she was just trying to frighten me, to teach me a lesson. But the mast shook in the wind, and I slipped off the platform. I reached out and felt a rope. I held it with hands as tight as a hare-hound's jaws. As I flapped around like a fish in a basket, I looked out over the sea. "Sail!" I cried. "I see a sail. Another ship!"

Ma ordered a small sailor, "Get up there and see what it is."

The man climbed like a monkey. He pushed me roughly back up into the crow's nest and joined me.

"English cog!" he shouted. "Trade ship.

Slow and low in the water. Fully loaded, I'd say, Ma'am. North by north-west, I reckon."

"Crew to attack stations!" Ma roared.

Men raced across the deck to haul out the cannon and collect weapons. The monkey-man helped me down to the deck.

My cold swim was forgotten.

Chapter Four
Whiskers and
Warships

Ma had a black flag hauled to the top of our mast. It was a sign to the other ship to stop or die.

The crew of the English ship lowered their sail. They knew it was no use trying to outrun us – they were too slow. They stood at the side rails and stared, sullen and afraid.

"I'm Grace O'Malley," Ma called across, "the greatest pirate that ever lived. We are coming alongside. We will take a share of your goods and not harm you," she promised. "What are you carrying?"

"Linen and woollen cloth. A little silk," an English sailor called back.

Ma grinned at me. "Silk, Catherine. You'll have a new dress when we get home."

"So you're not going to throw me in the sea?"

She shrugged. "Only if the ship is too crowded," she joked. At least, I think it was a joke.

It took most of the morning to carry the bales of cloth across. Slowly, the English ship grew lighter and rose, and ours sank lower. When the last of the cloth was on board, the cog sailed back to Plymouth and we turned around slowly.

Our ship was riding in the water like a fallen tree. "We'll be in Dublin this time tomorrow," Ma told the crew. "Our prize will fetch a good price in the market. And we didn't even have to sail to Spain."

A small man with the face of a mouse and a thin, whiskery beard stepped forward. I knew he was Seaman Michael Paterson. "Three cheers for Captain Grace O'Malley, Pirate Queen of Ireland. Hip, hip – "

"Ship ahead!" came a cry from the crow's nest.

The cheer from the crew died in their throats.

"We haven't room below deck to take any more loot," Ma called back. "Let it go."

"It's an English warship, Captain Grace. And it's heading this way," the lookout called.

"Set sail for Ireland!" Ma cried, and the crew raced to raise the sails. But now we were low in the water and heavy with that cloth. We were as slow as the cog we'd just robbed.

The English warship drew closer and we could see her sailors loading the cannon on the decks.

"What do we do, Captain?" Paterson moaned. "They have twenty guns, we have six. They'll blow us out of the water."

Grace O'Malley wrapped a large arm around his shoulder and grinned. "No, they won't, Seaman Paterson. No, they won't. Gather round, crew – I have a plan. After all, I *am* the greatest pirate that ever lived."

"Gather round, crew!" Paterson shouted. "Captain O'Malley has a wonderful plan to save us all."

When the sailors gathered on the deck, my ma spoke quietly over the sound of the slapping waves. "Now, lads, we're in a tight spot. But we're still alive. If we stand and fight, we'll probably die. So what I think we should do is surrender."

"No-o-o-o," Paterson moaned. "They'll take us back to Plymouth and hang us all. I'd rather die fighting."

Grace O'Malley shook her head. "These are English sailors, Michael. They have a way of doing things. It's the way of gentlemen. If we raise a white flag, they won't fire on us. Their captain will come on board and he will ask me to hand over my sword as a sign that we surrender."

"Then they'll take us on their ship and hang us."

"That is the gentleman's way," Grace nodded. "But we are not gentlemen. At least, *I'm* not."

The crew chuckled. "So what do we do?"

"When their captain climbs aboard our ship, we capture him. We say we'll cut his throat if they don't let us sail home to Dublin."

"Grace O'Malley, you're not just the greatest pirate in Ireland," Paterson laughed.

"No, no, no, Michael," grinned Ma. "I'm the greatest pirate the world has ever seen!"

Chapter Five
Flag and Fall

Ma told me to climb the mast and fasten a white flag at the top. Then I was to climb back down and hide in the cabin while our crew fought the English.

I tied the flag around my neck so my hands were free to climb. Before I reached the top, I saw the English sailors loading their cannon. The knot on the flag around my neck was tangled and my cold fingers were too numb to untie it.

First I saw a puff of grey smoke from the mouth of an English cannon. Moments later, I heard the sound of the explosion and then the splash as it landed in the water just in front of our bow.

"They missed," I muttered and suddenly the flag came free.

"Hurry up, child," Ma roared at me. "That was a warning shot. The next one will hit the mast and it'll be the end of you!"

"Wait!" I cried to the English ship, but my words were whipped away by the wind.

Ma waved a fist at me. "You, Catherine O'Malley, are a disgrace to the O'Malley name!"

"Sorry, Ma," I moaned, as I wrestled with the flapping flag.

"You're as much use as a comb on a bald man's head."

"I know, Ma," I muttered, as the flag at last flew free and fluttered in my face. I clung onto the crow's nest and watched as an Englishman in a fine red coat with golden buttons stepped onto the deck of the enemy ship.

"I am Captain Dudley of Her Majesty Queen Elizabeth's fleet," the man shouted over the whipping water.

"Good for you," Ma snorted.

"I'm going to cross to your ship and take your sword as a sign of your surrender," he went on as the English frigate lowered its sails and let the wind drift it towards our side. I climbed halfway down the mast, till I was just over my ma's head.

I heard her speak softly to the crew, "He'll get my sword all right – in the throat, if I have my way."

Old Hugh O'Neil stepped forward. "Kill Captain Dudley and they'll blow us out of the water," he warned. "We need to take him prisoner, then they won't dare fire on us."

"I know that, I know that, old man," Ma snapped.

Everyone on the ship seemed to hold their breath as the English sailors threw a rope with a hook onto our deck and fastened our ships together.

They placed a plank between the ships and we watched as the English captain climbed onto our ship.

The Englishman was so fat the buttons on his red coat were bursting. But I wasn't looking at the gleaming gold buttons so much as the polished pistol he held in his hand.

"We've been waiting years to capture you, Grace O'Malley," he said. "Queen Elizabeth has heard of your evil robbing ways."

"Is that right?" Ma laughed. "What an honour for me to be so popular with old Queen Bess."

"Hand over your sword," Captain Dudley said, and jabbed his pistol towards her.

I could see Ma's plan would never work. If she tried to jump at him with her sword, he would fire his pistol and kill her. Then I remembered the tale she'd told in the draughty hall of the castle. I was clinging to the mast, just above his pistol arm.

I let go and fell towards him.

At that very moment, Ma decided to make a grab for the captain's pistol. She jumped forward. Dudley jumped back. I landed on Ma's head. She fell forward and cracked her head on the deck. She gave a soft groan and the light in her eyes went out.

Chapter Six
Richmond and Ruffs

The English captain had my ma carried across to his ship. Seaman Michael Paterson jumped forward and pushed his mouse face close to Captain Dudley. I thought he was going to fight and die for Ma.

But he just whined, "Oh, Captain, sir, we are so very happy to be free of the pirate queen! We've been her slaves for years."

The rest of the black-hearted crew began to nod and agree to Paterson's lies.

"Let us go free," the little seaman snuffled. "We'll go back to our old mothers and our weeping wives. We'll never set foot on a pirate ship again. If we do, you can cut off the feet that touch the decks. Isn't that right, lads?"

"Aye," they agreed.

Captain Dudley looked around and his long, fine nose sniffed the air as if he were smelling rats. He was. "It's Grace O'Malley we want. I haven't room on my ship to arrest the lot of you. Clear off back to Ireland."

The crew hurried across the decks to set sail for freedom. I ran after Captain Dudley. "I want to go with my ma!" I told him.

The man just shrugged and nodded.

Ma was fastened in chains and put in the captain's cabin. She woke as we set sail along the coast of England. "What happened?" she muttered, rubbing her head.

"Something fell on top of you," I said.

Before she could ask, the cabin door opened and Captain Dudley walked in. "Well, Grace O'Malley, Queen Elizabeth herself has asked to see you before we hang you. The Queen of England wants to meet the Queen of the Pirates."

"It's a great honour," Ma said coldly. "An honour for Elizabeth, that is," she added.

"We'll be at Tilbury dock tomorrow morning," said the man. "Here's some bread and cheese for you and the girl." Then he left.

Ma grinned. "Not just bread and cheese, Catherine, my dear. But a knife to cut it with. A knife I plan to plunge into the heart of Queen Elizabeth, if the woman has a heart."

"No, Ma! They'll kill you if you try."

"They plan to hang me anyway," she argued. "I may as well take that Tudor witch with me."

And nothing I could say would change her mind.

Ma had slipped the knife into her boot, and next day we rattled over the rutted roads of London to Greenwich Palace. Crowds were waiting at the gate.

"They've come to see the greatest pirate in the world," Ma laughed, and waved at the people.

We were led across a courtyard and through a door that was big enough to make a Connacht ship. The hall was crowded with gentlemen in satin jackets of more colours than a rainbow and ruffs as big as cartwheels. The ladies were in silk but in dull shades of brown and black.

Ma leaned towards me and whispered, "See? The queen doesn't like ladies to shine brighter than her."

"No, Ma," I said.

We stood in front of an empty throne and Ma looked around. "Have you all had a good look, you English peacocks?" she shouted. "You can tell your children you've seen the greatest pirate in the world."

Suddenly, a door behind the throne opened and the people in the court bowed very low. The Queen of England walked in.

Chapter Seven
Teeth and Tales

Queen Elizabeth walked slowly. Her ugly face was painted white, and red powder was brushed on her lips and cheeks. Her little black eyes glittered like wet coal and she hobbled under the weight of her dress, which was crusted with jewels.

While everyone except Ma had their heads bowed to the floor, I dropped to my knees. With a quick flick,

I'd raised Ma's skirt and pulled the knife out of her boot.

Queen Elizabeth frowned. "You should curtsey before your queen."

Ma gave a secret smile and bent her knees in a deep curtsey. I watched as she swept back her hand and felt in her boot for the knife. Her hand jerked upwards and she cried out, "Aieeee!", her killing scream.

She looked at the empty hand. She blushed. She gave a giggle. "Er... I... er... eeee... er... oh, my knees... my *knees*. The old bones hurt these days," she mumbled, to cover her foolish cry.

The English queen nodded. "I know, my dear, I have the same problem. My doctor gives me some good ointment made from goose grease. I'll get my maids to fetch you some."

"It will be a great comfort when you hang me from the gallows tomorrow."

Elizabeth looked at Ma, curious. "So you're the pirate I've heard so much about."

"And you're the queen I've heard a bit about. You're not very tall, are you?"

I heard a gasp from the crowd at my ma's cheek. The old queen smiled and showed black and broken teeth. "I haven't got my father's massive body, but I do have his huge heart, Grace O'Malley, and that's what counts in a queen. You should know that."

Ma nodded. "That's true, Bess," she said.

No one in the room seemed to breathe.

"How did you get into the pirate trade?" the queen asked. She sat on her throne and patted her ginger wig straight. "Sit by my side and tell me."

Ma moved to the seat by the throne and began her old tale. "It all started with my father. A big, bullying brute of a man."

"Same as my father... King Henry the Eighth... though we used to call him Henry the *Ate*, he grew so fat!"

For the rest of that morning, my ma told her tales of piracy and the fights she'd had. The queen asked some questions, but mostly she listened like a child at the feet of her nurse.

When the midday sun shone high in the sky, we were led off to a small room at the side of the throne room to eat. And at the end of the day, the weary old queen said, "It has been a pleasure to meet you, Grace."

Ma sighed. "And it will be your pleasure to hang me in the morning."

"Hang you? Goodness me, no! The sign of a great queen is this – you should know when to be cruel and when to show mercy.

And I am showing mercy to you, Grace O'Malley. Go back to Ireland and your family."

Ma blinked. "You're setting me free?"

"I am," Old Queen Bess said with a smile. "Rest here tonight and I'll have a ship sail you back to Connacht tomorrow."

Chapter Eight
Freedom and Feathers

Ma gave the queen a wide smile. "You really do have a heart as big as a horse."

The queen limped to the door, stopped and looked back. "Of course, if I catch you attacking any more English ships, I'll hang you from the tallest tree in Ireland."

"Of course," Ma said. "What about Spanish and Scottish ships?"

"Oh, help yourself to those!" Elizabeth chuckled. She waved a pale hand wrapped in a cloud of jewels and was gone.

Ma ruffled my hair. "She's not such a bad old bird, after all."

"No, Ma."

"In fact, I'm rather glad I didn't kill her when I had the chance."

"Me too, Ma."

"I wonder what in the devil's name happened to that knife?" she muttered.

I felt the blade hard under the back of my belt where I'd pushed it. "I wonder, Ma."

Servants led the way to a fine room in the palace and I climbed into the soft, goose-feather bed next to my ma.

"I like this," she said as she lay back sleepily. "Maybe we'll rob a ship that has a goose-feather bed on board, eh, Catherine?"

"No, Ma, you need to give up pirating," I moaned. "If the Spanish catch you, they won't forgive you like Queen Bess did."

Ma gave a long sigh. "You're right, Catherine, you're right. But it would be a terrible pity to retire when I'm the greatest pirate the world has ever seen."

"Yes, Ma," I said, and fell asleep in the arms of the greatest ma the world has ever seen.

Epilogue

In this story Catherine is made up. Grace O'Malley (born around 1530) was real. She was the Pirate Queen of Connacht with three galleys and 200 warriors. She cut her hair short so she could sail with her father. That's probably how she got her nickname Granuaile, which means "bald".

Her father always refused to let her sail with him, so she had to hide on one of his ships. Her first husband, Donal, was a pirate on the west coast of Ireland. When he died, she took over his fleet of ships.

She was hated by the English, who ruled Ireland, and they set out to arrest her.

Grace also took over her second husband's castle. She was trapped there by an English army. She took lead from the roof, melted it and poured the boiling lead on the English heads to drive them away. When her father died, she took over his fleet, too. She began to raid England and Scotland as well as Ireland.

In 1593, she went to London to meet Queen Elizabeth. The two women were about the same age – around 60 – when they met at Greenwich Palace.

Grace wore a fine gown, but had a dagger hidden on her person. Guards found it before she could attack the queen. Grace said she was carrying the dagger to defend herself. Queen Elizabeth believed her.

Grace refused to bow before Elizabeth because, she said, Elizabeth wasn't the Queen of Ireland. Still, Elizabeth liked Grace O'Malley and set her free. Grace said she would stop her rebel raids and Elizabeth said she would stop the English soldiers attacking Grace's castles. But Grace broke her promise and soon went back to her wicked ways.

Both women died in the year 1603.

TERRY DEARY'S TALES